THE
MOURNING
DOVE

THE
MOURNING
DOVE

A STORY OF LOVE

LARRY BARKDULL

Golden Books

NEW YORK

Golden Books®
888 Seventh Avenue
New York, NY 10106

Copyright © 1996, 1997 by Barkdull Publishing, LLC

Portions of this book were adapted from "The Prodigal," a
short story by Larry Barkdull and Marvin Payne. The story of
the grateful cat in the chapter "Oscar, I Love You" was adapted
from an allegory by James E. Talmage in the magazine
Improvement Era, August 1916, pages 875–876. Although the
author has drawn extensively from personal experiences, all
characters and situations are fictitious.

Typography: Title in Cirrus, Text in Weiss
Illustrations by Yan Nascimbene

Library of Congress Cataloging-in-Publication Data
Barkdull, Larry.
The mourning dove : a story of love / Larry Barkdull.
p.   cm.
ISBN 0-307-44011-7 (hc : alk. paper)
I. Title.
PS3552.A6166M69   1997
813' .54–dc21
97-6792   CIP   ISBN 0–307–44011–7

Printed in Italy

SPECIAL THANKS

To Cheryl and Brian Crouch and the booksellers of
southeast Idaho who helped launch this book.
To Jerry Garrett, Ron Hansen, Alan and Suzanne Osmond,
Jennifer Christiansen, Sandy Dalrymple, and Pat Sheranian.

To my agent, Jan Miller, and the incredible
staff of Dupree, Miller & Associates.

To Bob, Cassie, Laura, Lori, Tiffany, and Ellen
of Golden Books.
Thanks for believing.

✄

For Elizabeth, who has blessed me these ten times

CONTENTS

May I not be judged too harshly. With each penned word, I longed for the literary prowess of greater talents. Still, this is a story I must tell.

❦

A New Home

I WAS NAMED HANNIBAL for the small town on the Mississippi that was central to my grandfather's favorite book, *Tom Sawyer*.

Early spring tulips were awakening through the stubborn winter's snow of 1959 when I first moved to my grandfather's home. I had just turned nine. We were well suited to one another—he had lost my grandmother some three years earlier, and I had been orphaned only three days. There seemed a certain warmth to his home—a kind of security I especially needed at that confusing time.

I shared my grandfather's last name—Huish—inherited from my father, his second son. My grandfather's given name was Porter—"Port" to his friends—but I called him "Pop." I hadn't made it up. He had insisted. I expect that others of my older cousins—some fifty—had coined the name. Whatever the origin, it had stuck, and Pop and I became fast friends.

Pop had led a long and varied working life. He had farmed, worked construction, and been employed briefly as a deputy sheriff. But since his retirement he sold brooms—industrial brooms—to car mechanics, maintenance men, and the sort. At nine, I imagined that this was a career I might pursue someday—either that or a career as a professional fisherman.

Twice a week Pop and I would load his pickup with brooms and work the circuit of the industrial areas on the outskirts of Boise. When we arrived at a familiar client's establishment, Pop would holler into the shop, "Broom man's here!" Maybe others would have used a more conventional approach. Still, invariably, the workmen would eagerly emerge from their grease pits, greet the old man—an indisputable friend—small-talk a while, and, of course, leave with new brooms.

Pop was born and reared in the backwoods hill country of Arkansas—the town of Gurdon in Clark County. A little rough and unrefined, but fully loveable and jolly, he measured just under six feet tall, was big-boned, a little overweight, and hobbled on a cane in his later years. Pop sported a full head of wavy white hair that he usually covered with a felt hat when he went out in public. In his later years he wore an equally white beard that he kept neatly trimmed. Grandmother, also from Arkansas, felt awkward about her accent when they had moved north, so she labored most of her life to lose it. Pop never did. That was both a delight and a comfort to me, for my first year in his home was filled with frequent nightmares that brought his southernly punctuated stories to my bedside. Not a few of my fondest rememberings are those of when I slipped into sleep in his ample arms as he spun stories of his boyhood in Gurdon.

Pop was a storyteller, or, as he would say, a yarn spinner. His yarns were usually preceded by face-pulling contests. Pop always won. My tries paled in comparison to his grotesque expressions. Of course, he had years of advantage in growing a perfectly pliable face accentuated by a huge, reddish nose. I have heard that the nose and ears grow throughout life. Pop's were living proof. I never stood a chance. Pop owned all the material to win any face-pulling competition. When the duel was decided, he would routinely recline in his rocker and for a moment stare off victoriously somewhere distant. At length, the corners of his mouth would turn up as if he was already laughing at what he was about to recite. Then, a tale from Gurdon would unfold.

Pop's tiny home was neatly kept. It had two bed-rooms—his and mine—a small kitchen, a living room with a fireplace and a television (which was always tuned to *Gunsmoke, Bonanza,* or some other western), and a forbidding basement housing the coal furnace. I didn't go down there. I was certain highwaymen and murderers habitually snuck in through the downstairs window and made the basement their hideout. It was a sure place to lose one's life, I figured. The groaning sounds of the furnace neither relieved my anxiety nor heightened my curiosity to explore the dark cavern.

My interest was piqued, however, by an object situated high above the fireplace. In the well-lighted living room, on the fireplace mantel, lay a beautifully carved oak box. I expected that it was at least special and maybe precious. It was never discussed and never opened—except that when I had once asked, Pop said it held a treasure. The box was displayed in full view like a fine piece of art. The delicate inlay and the precision of each raised design had obviously required skilled workmanship. Its hinges stretched across the lid like the slender stems of a young willow, and it locked in the front with a golden hasp. It was positioned just out of my reach but not out of my wonderment. That fascination would one day prove nearly lethal, and give me the greatest lesson of my life.

Although Pop and I had fun, Pop's was still a quiet neighborhood for a nine-year-old boy. Most of his neighbors were his age. Still, large maples, vacant lots, and local fields provided sufficient opportunity for a small boy to occupy long hours without a playmate. Sometimes Pop and I fished the surrounding rivers and lakes for which Idaho is famous. After each trip, Pop would prepare the fish the Arkansas way and we would feast.

We didn't hunt, although Pop owned a twelve-gauge shotgun. Pop figured that killing for sport brought out the worst in a man, that animals should be reverently observed and allowed to be safe in their habitats. At nine I didn't agree, but my begging didn't change things. I had heard Pop tell the stories of his youth when he had raised hounds and hunted raccoons by moonlight. I wanted the same, but Pop's was no longer a killing constitution. I suppose because of my obsessive fascination the hunting stories stopped altogether.

One summer's evening as I hung by my heels from a branch of a massive maple tree, I caught my trousers on a spiked limb and fell to the ground, landing on the side of my head. When I awoke I was screaming for my mother. Pop was at my side in an instant. He gathered me into his arms and carried me into the house. He soon discovered that I was bruised but not damaged. Still, he knew that because I had hit my head I should not immediately go to sleep. So, into the night he talked me awake.

Late in the evening our conversation grew reflective. "I saw Mom and Dad in their caskets," I said. "They looked just the same, but they didn't move."

Pop looked off somewhere. "I remember."

"Pop, where do people go when they die?"

"I believe they go back to God, who gave them life," he said.

"Do they look the same, then?"

"I think so."

"I sometimes forget what they looked like and what they sounded like. Do you think they have forgotten me?"

"No, Hannibal," Pop replied quietly. "That love goes on and on."

"What if I forget them?"

"You never forget the ones who gave you life and loved you perfectly."

"Pop, you won't die, will you?" I asked. I curled into his generous lap and he held me into the night.

◆ ◆ ◆

JOHNSON, GO PREACH!

POP HAD SAT SERIOUSLY for as long as he could stand it. I sensed something was happening when I heard him chuckle to himself.

"What's so funny?" I asked.

"Did I ever tell you how Ol' Man Johnson got called to the ministry?" Of course he had, but I pretended he hadn't.

"No, Pop. Tell me," I urged.

A peculiarity of his natural southern drawl was that it thickened when he told stories from his youth.

"Well, sir, back in Gurdon, the little town where I grew up, our neighbor, Ol' Man Johnson, had just bought hisself a right fine old mule, and he swore that old thing could communicate. My pa didn't believe it, of course, but allowed a feller the right to act stupid if he had a mind to. I never seen a body so attached to a dumb animal as ol' Johnson. Why, Miz Johnson got right irritated at him for spendin' so much time with the critter, and complained real forceful of his continual neglect. Well, he couldn't understand none of her cluckin' because her mouth was full of new store-bought false teeth, and they wasn't broke in good yet. And even though he was right curious about what she had to say, he took more particular interest in how them teeth clacked in her head every time she opened her mouth. This got her all the more excited, and when she started jaw flappin' again, those contraptions dropped plumb out of her mouth and landed right at his feet. He told her it was disgusting for a wife to spit her teeth at her husband like that, and went off to talk to the mule. Well, she gummed a response to him that could be heard halfway 'cross the county, to the effect that he would have to make a choice between her and the mule. It must have been no contest, 'cause she moved out that very next mornin' and ain't been heard from since.

"Now, Ol' Man Johnson was real religious. He attended every prayer meeting that come around each summer, and he confessed quite regular. Me and my friends sat nearby and looked on, but never participated—we just chalked it up to a fine evening of entertainment since we didn't have television and such. On occasion, the spirit fell on ol' Johnson and he'd speak in tongues. So did the mule, he claimed.

"After one such meeting, he became remarkably animated and loaded up the mule with tracts. Well, sir, bright and early the next mornin' we were roused upright, straight out of our beds, to the wild rantin's of ol' Johnson.

" 'Huish! Joseph Huish!'—that were my pa—'come on out here!' Well, sir, my pa ran right to the window to see what all the ruckus was about and why Ol' Man Johnson was bawlin' so. Well, Pa tried to calm the ol' fool for fear of his faintin' dead away and having to administer mouth-to-mouth.

" 'Come on in here and set a minute, Amos,' Pa said.

"Well, he come in, but there weren't no settin'.

" 'Joseph,' says ol' Johnson, his arms a-flappin', 'Joseph, I've been called to the ministry!'

" 'What's that?' Pa says.

" 'If I'm lyin' may I be struck dumb!' says Johnson.

"We expected it had happened already, but we listened on.

" 'This mornin',' says Johnson, 'real early, I goes out to feed my mule. Well, sir, you're not going to believe this'—and I didn't—'that mule looks me right in the eye, sits back on his two hind legs, raises the front two up in the air, and brays some words at me.' "

Now, at this part of the story Pop threw back

his head and mimicked the braying animal, saying
" 'Jaaawhnson . . . go preeeach! Go preeeach! Go preeeach!' "

Pop and I hooted until we cried. Neither of us
could stop. And so it went for the rest of the night, one
yarn after another, bawling our eyes out, and howling
with laughter until we ached.

Those were gentle times that I unfold whenever
adult life becomes very serious. I quietly step back into
evenings filled with yarns, moments of complete giddi-
ness, and face-pulling contests. And, for a moment, I am
again a small boy in the hearth of my grandfather's love.

◆ ◆ ◆

THE SILENCING

CHARLIE BENNETT CAME TO our neighborhood one June morning just when school had ended. Charlie was two years my senior, but had been kept back a grade. Even with our age difference we found in each other the companionship that we needed. That summer we mainly played outdoors. Charlie invited me to his house only once. I soon discovered why.

Charlie lived alone with his father. When I first met him, Mr. Bennett ignored his son's introduction of his newfound friend, cursed a foul oath, and disappeared behind a bedroom door. The dwelling was a ramshackle shack, dark and dirty, and smelled distinctly of liquor. Charlie appeared embarrassed and suggested that we play outdoors. I didn't disagree.

Henry Bennett was perhaps the most frightening character I had ever encountered. He stunk of sweat and filth. His loathsome, unshaven face framed a crooked nose that had been broken at least once, but never set. A jagged scar was set just below his unkempt, greasy black hair and above his right eyebrow. Sometimes Charlie wore the welts and bruises from disciplinings, but he always shrugged them off as accidents. Still, Charlie paled when Mr. Bennett hollered for him. Usually we would crouch together in some secluded spot until his father melted back into the shadows of the shack.

Pop said I needn't fear the miserable fellow, that I should just leave him alone and be a good friend to Charlie. His counsel was wise, and, left to ourselves, Charlie and I played as happily as two boys ever did. Still, Mr. Bennett's dark figure staring from his shaded window did not relieve my anxiety.

In those days, Boise was a mixture of residential and rural dwellings situated side by side. Our neighbors, Mr. and Mrs. Davies, owned a small five-acre farm. They had a horse, some chickens and pigs, and a Jersey cow named Gertrude that Mr. Davies milked twice each day. They allowed us boys to feed the animals and help with small chores. Mr. Davies even let us try to milk Gertrude once. Her discomfort decided our destiny as dairymen. Yet Charlie's and my failure as milkers was forgiven—at least by the Davieses—and we were allowed free rein of their farm. I suppose the old couple saw in us boys the grandsons they had been denied. In any case, we were treated like family and, in time, Charlie and I were each given a calf to rear. I named mine *Oscar* and Charlie named his *Meyer*.

Those were happy times. Pop didn't mind that I had found a friend in Charlie. He let me live my boyhood with little restraint, only occasionally pulling in the reins as situations demanded.

Oscar and Meyer occupied a pen just below the haystack where Charlie and I built a towering fort. At twenty bales high, it allowed us to survey most of our neighborhood and pick up an occasional cooling breeze that softened the sweltering summer days. Beginning at the bottom of the haystack, we had managed to build a series of tunnels that serpentined their way to the fort above. One tunnel led to a lower balcony, where we played King of Bunker's Hill. The rules were simple— the one on top of the hill of bales remained king unless his challenger could dethrone him by pushing him off. I mostly lost because of my inferior size and age. But Charlie usually granted me a boon, as a true friend does, and allowed me ample regal privilege. Then on sleepy afternoons we retired to lie in irrigation ditches, soaking our poor bodies to escape the midday heat.

Charlie hunted. He liked it. Oddly, it was one activity he could share with his father. Charlie had a

•

.22-caliber rifle. It was long and beautiful. Pop didn't know that we boys toyed with it or that I had shot it at bottles and tree limbs. Charlie wanted more. "Let's go hunting for real," he would say. I knew how Pop felt, so I always made an excuse. Still, the idea intrigued me. I could picture myself as a natural hunter—as if I was born for it.

Each day, when I returned from play, I would sneak to the top of the stairs that led to the furnace room and gaze longingly at the closed closet below where Pop's shotgun was kept. I would have crept down to examine it closely except for its disquieting location. Nothing was worth that.

Charlie's pesterings continued and soon my resolve weakened. For several days I rehearsed in my mind just how I could ask Pop to go hunting and have it sound legitimate. At length, I had it—the crows were eating all the crops in the fields, I reasoned, and I had to stop them. It sounded plausible. I could imagine that Pop would agree and want me to march right out there and fix things with his gun. I would ask at dinner that night.

Brussels sprouts were not my favorite, but they cyclically appeared on my plate. This was one of those times. I chased them around with a fork a while, then decided that maybe a diversion would help.

"Pop," I started, "have you seen all the crows this year?"

"Can't say that I've taken much notice," he said, plopping another sprout in his mouth like nothing was wrong.

"Well, they're eating everything! Soon there won't be anything left."

Pop looked up. I think he knew where this was headed.

"We've got to do something. Can't we hunt them just this once—to save the fields, I mean?" There. I had said it.

Pop leaned back in his chair and studied me a moment. "Charlie's got a gun, hasn't he?"

I hesitated. "Just a little one."

"And he hunts?"

"Well, I think he has a couple of times . . . with his dad."

Pop eyed me a little more. "You really think the crows will get the best of those fields?"

"Oh, yes, Pop!" I blurted out. "When you see what they've done—"

"Okay," he interrupted, motioning me to finish the last two brussels sprouts on my plate, "first thing in the morning we'll get my gun and chase away those pesky birds."

I couldn't believe it had been so easy, but I didn't dare let on. My first hunting trip! I knew I wouldn't sleep that night. I was right.

Early the next morning I was in Pop's room rousting him out of bed. "Time to go!" I urged.

"It can wait a bit," he mumbled. "Why don't you go get the gun and make us some breakfast?"

Get the gun? That would mean I would have to descend to the furnace room to fetch it.

"You're right, Pop," I conceded. "We'd better eat first."

Old people don't move very fast, I decided. Pop took his time in the bathroom; he mulled over his morning's paper; he breakfasted leisurely; then he even brushed his teeth!

"Come on, Pop!" I begged. "Look at the sun. The crows will all be gone."

Ultimately, he yielded to my fussing and descended the stairs to fetch the twelve gauge.

I held my breath until Pop reappeared from the dark cellar. Thank goodness he was safe. He opened the double-barreled chamber to see that it was empty, then handed the gun to me. "Okay," he said, "let's go."

The shotgun weighed more than I had imagined. It was awkward, too. Pop soon saw my dilemma and showed me how to carry the shotgun by folding my arms underneath and draping the barrel over my right forearm. That repositioning made the hike tolerable.

I was thrilled as we neared the predesignated

cornfield. We had arrived! I began scanning the terrain and skies for any unsuspecting crows. With all my plotting, I had actually convinced myself that the crows really did pose a threat. I have often wondered at the power of the mind to believe a lie when the desire is strong enough.

We began at one end of a cornfield and traversed its length by following the furrows. Then, when we reached its outer boundary, we turned and forded the ocean of yellow again. By the third trip it had become painfully clear that no crows were to be found. We trekked around a bit more, but soon gave up.

At length Pop said, "Let's sit a while." We located a big shade tree and rested our backs against it.

"You're disappointed, aren't you?" he observed. I was, but I didn't answer. "Here, let me show you a few things you need to know about a gun." So, for the next half hour I learned the shotgun, each detail, every feature. With Pop's aid I aimed at various targets and pulled the trigger. Click! The chambers were empty, but I pretended otherwise. Soon, when he was satisfied I was amusing myself, Pop settled back, pulled his hat over his face, and drifted off to sleep.

Maybe ten minutes passed, maybe fifteen. I don't recall. Abruptly, to my left I thought I saw something small scurry through the brush, then freeze. I slowly turned my head. Nothing. I remained perfectly still. Only the sounds of Pop's gentle breathing disturbed the late morning air. There it was again, a rustling, but I saw nothing. I strained my eyes but dared not move. Another minute passed. Then, suddenly, when it thought itself safe, a grayish brown bird with a tinge of pink on its breast appeared on the top of a fence post about thirty feet in front of me.

It wasn't a crow. I had never seen anything quite like it before. Just as certainly I knew that this would be my last hunting trip with Pop. Trouble was, Pop was sleeping right through it, and I didn't dare wake him for fear my prey might take flight.

It wasn't hard to decide what to do. Almost in slow motion I inched my hand toward the shotgun. I gingerly dragged the weapon to my side, then reached inside Pop's vest pocket for a shotgun shell. I loaded the magazine just as Pop had shown me. I then carefully closed the chamber and released the safety. Easily I lay front-side down on the soft earth, and quietly raised the gun until it rested on a large stone. I moved the shotgun back and forth, up and down, until I could view the bird squarely along the barrel, its head dead center in the bead of the sight. I took a deep breath and exhaled slowly. Suddenly, I saw the bird straighten in alarm and turn in my direction. An incredible explosion kicked me backward and a terrible pain sliced through my right shoulder. Pop startled to his feet.

"Hannibal! What happened? Are you hurt?"

I lay there dumbfounded a moment, gaping at the smoking gun in front of me and the empty fence post beyond. My shock turned to euphoria. "I did it, Pop!" I screamed in delight. "I shot a bird!"

Pop was stunned. As quickly as he picked me up and dusted me off, I broke his hold and sprinted to the fence post to gather my trophy. Pop removed the cartridge and followed. He said nothing. I fumbled around in the brush, then stopped cold when I stumbled on a clump of feathers and the limp body of a beautiful bird. It measured about ten inches long, with a slender beak and darkish tail feathers with a white border. I knelt down and gently scooped up its corpse in my hands. Something warm dripped from between my fingers as the bird's long neck hung lifeless and slack. I tried to turn toward Pop and look victorious, but I was sick.

Pop stayed his distance. "It's a mourning dove," he said. "Probably has a nest nearby."

He was right. On the ground, under a bush, camouflaged and concealed, yet given away by their crying, lay two hungry chicks with just the hint of pinfeathers. I moved closer. They weren't afraid of me; they hadn't learned. As I stretched out my hand, the larger chick puffed out his chest and struck at me with his beak. His feisty defense of his nest and nestmate was admirable.

"Don't touch them, Hannibal," Pop cautioned. "One of them might have a chance if their father will raise it alone." The terrible truth cut deep into my heart like a hot dagger—I had killed their mother!

"You've got a choice to make," Pop said as he squeezed my shoulder. I knew what he meant, but couldn't believe I was in this situation. In his way, Pop was telling me that one of the chicks had to die if either was to have a chance to live. I slowly bent down to the chicks, then looked up to Pop for help. But he wisely held back and let the moment weigh on me. Tears welled up in my eyes as I picked up one of the chicks and held it in my hand. I whispered to it and wept in grief for what I was about to do.

I turned to Pop with a tear-streaked face and showed him the chick in my cupped hand. "This one," I said. I knew Pop wouldn't help; I knew he shouldn't. He gave me a suggestion about how to do the deed swiftly and painlessly.

When I had finished, Pop was holding the dead mother. "You want to take her home?" Pop asked knowingly.

"No, Pop," I replied softly as tears filled my eyes again. "I'd like to bury her here with her baby."

We fashioned a shallow grave close to their nest

and placed them in it together. The mother dove's blood had stained my hands and I couldn't rub it off. Pop's silence spoke a poignant lesson I have not since forgotten. When we were through, Pop shouldered the shotgun, put his arm around me, and guided me home. In the distance I heard the mournful cooing of a mate left alone.

◆ ◆ ◆

WITH A SILKEN THREAD

TUESDAYS AND FRIDAYS WERE broom-selling days. Much before dawn, on the last Tuesday of June, Pop shook me from my bed to help him load his pickup with brooms, tools, and, oddly, groceries. "What're these for?" I asked, pointing at the boxes of food.

"We've got an early stop to make in Caldwell before we go selling," he replied. The tiny township of Caldwell was one of my favorite places. Some of my cousins resided in the rural areas outside the little town. When my family lived in neighboring Nampa, I saw my cousins often. Some four months had passed since the last time, though.

"Are we going to Aunt Floy's?" I pressed, hopeful.

"Not this time," Pop answered. "But you've got a second cousin there named Jillian."

I laid my sleepy head on Pop's lap as he pulled onto the highway that led to Caldwell. The spinning of the truck's tires was the only sound that disturbed the still, dark night. We traveled the road alone. Except for the truck's headlights, only the faint glimmer of the moon could be seen through the trees. Suddenly, we passed the trees and I rousted myself to a beautiful sight.

"Pop! Look at that!" I stuck my finger on the windshield, pointing at the bright yellow moon hovering low in the sky.

"Pretty, isn't it?" he commented.

I gazed on it as we drove into the early morning. "Why is there a moon?" I asked.

"You tell me," Pop replied.

"For light?" I guessed.

"That's right," he commended me. "When God made the earth he also made all the great lights in the heavens: the moon, the stars, and the sun. Because of the sun's light, plants grow and we live. The sun's light is like God's great love for us—it falls on us in abundance, it warms us, it makes all life possible. When we walk in its light we can see where we're going so we won't fall. Sometimes we turn from the light just like the earth turns from the sun, and we find ourselves in darkness. But the moon shines through the darkness with the reflected light of the sun and illuminates our way to morning.

"Look over there," he said, pointing to a brilliant star on the eastern horizon. "That's the morning star."

"It's so bright!" I replied almost reverently.

We both watched it a while as the pickup moved quietly over the smooth asphalt. Pop said, "When you go out tonight, just before the sun sets, look to the West and you will see it again. Then it will be called the evening star. It has two important jobs: in the evening it climbs the sky like a watchman on a tower guarding his sleeping children. Then the moon appears, bathing the world in its soft glow as it traverses the heavens. And when the night is most dark and deep, the morning star rises heralding the promise of morning. I've always thought that God made the moon and the stars to remind us that when life is the darkest we are never alone. We have but to look up and his light is always there."

I gazed out the windshield at the bright moon and the morning star spilling their light on my welcome face. I thought about Pop's words. I could see the distant beams of the sun's warm rising ushering in the morning.

As we entered Caldwell, Pop explained about Jillian. I didn't know what an unwed mother was or why her family would shut her out. Pop said her tiny baby had been sick for two weeks with the croup. Jillian lacked food and medicine, and someone to care.

I had seen Pop do this before, usually anonymously. Because he had slowed in his old age, I was often the one who delivered the boxes of oranges, winter coats, envelopes of cash, or other offerings. I had become quite adept at sneaking up to porches, depositing surprises, ringing doorbells, and sprinting away. Other times, only a compassionate visit and a clean handkerchief were required. Pop kept a clean one handy.

When we arrived at her little rundown shack, Jillian was waiting at the front door as if she were expecting us, holding her crying child. Pop sent me to fetch the food while he stepped inside with the wisp of a girl. She looked more my age than she did a mother. When I had set the boxes in the kitchen, I saw that Pop had produced a small bottle from his pocket and was explaining to Jillian how often and how much to give the baby.

Jillian quieted as I entered the room. I felt awkward and self-conscious. "What's his name?" I asked, pointing to the child on her lap.

"Thomas," she replied, "for my father. And yours is Hannibal?"

"Yes," I said, kneeling by the baby.

"You want to hold him?" she asked.

I looked up at Pop, who nodded his approval. "Hold your arms like this," she demonstrated. Then she handed Thomas to me. I thought at first I might drop him, but Pop steadied me with his hand under mine. I had never seen anything so beautiful. Thomas's little hand wrapped around my thumb with surprising strength, and he cooed something soft at me.

"Where's his dad?" I asked without thinking.

Pop cleared his throat in my direction, but Jillian didn't mind. "He's not with us any longer. It's just me and Thomas now."

I sat in the truck while Pop and Jillian good-byed. I saw him reach into his pocket and squeeze an envelope into her reluctant hand. She wept openly on his broad shoulder and kissed his cheek. As we drove away I thought I saw tears well in Pop's eyes. I looked away and didn't mention them.

⚬

"It's time we stopped in Nampa," Pop said. "I need to find some papers in your old house. You can stay in the truck if you don't want to come in." I had fifteen minutes to decide as we drove the country roads that led to Nampa. I didn't know how to feel. When we parked in front of the house, I just sat a moment, resting my chin on my folded arms that draped over the pickup's open window. When Pop stepped from the driver's side I decided I would follow him inside.

Our yard looked as it always had, except the long grass lay clumped and matted from lack of mowing.

Someone had placed a big padlock on the front door. But Pop had a key and soon we were in. A distinct musty smell permeated the house, and rays of light marked the dusty air. Outside of hurriedly gathering my belongings, Pop and I had not returned to clean, organize, or sell the house. His whole attention was given to my settling with him and his comforting me.

Mom and Dad left nothing. At their poor, young age they had struggled just to buy this old "fixer-upper" that Dad worked on most evenings. Mom had recently started painting the kitchen area, and she had stored some carpet remnants in a corner to replace the worn one in my bedroom.

Twenty-nine is not a fair time to die. The weekend vacation they had planned for so long was cut short in a freak accident when their car slid out of control on an icy highway. They were to have brought me a surprise.

Pop and I looked over the old house for evidence of a life insurance policy, supposedly squirreled away somewhere, which might defray some of their burial expenses. If one existed, the face value wouldn't be much—maybe a thousand dollars. Dad, when they were newly married, had purchased a single premium life insurance policy on himself for the death benefit. The policy had a savings feature, and if they hadn't cashed it in for home repairs, it might still be here, stashed securely away.

What an empty scene lay before me! The house held all the evidences of life: the bunched-up pillow against the back of Dad's favorite armchair; the cracker crumbs left on the kitchen table; a list of relatives' names and numbers taped to the wall by the phone. Nothing had been disturbed since March fifth. It all appeared so normal that I expected Mom and Dad to enter the room at any moment and greet me with a smile and a hug.

I fought back the tears. I'm one of those *big* criers—I save it up, then, when I can hold it no longer, I gush all over the place. I hurried back to help Pop find the policy.

Maybe in a desk drawer. I couldn't believe what a person could collect in twenty-something years. I caught myself taking mental pictures of each piece of paraphernalia, which yesterday seemed so trivial, but today, collectively, summed up my parents' lives. Everything appeared important, even the little scraps of paper they used for making notes.

In one drawer Pop found some documents in a folder simply labeled HOUSE. Inside lay the carefully folded mortgage papers on our home and a handwritten table showing year by year how the balance would decrease. A thorough search produced nothing else of consequence except a card resting on the desktop—

addressed to me.

Pop stuffed the mortgage papers in his pocket and I reached for the card. "May your pain pass quickly," it read. It hadn't worked. I knew the friend had meant well, but the wish hung hollow like other well-wishers' "It was a blessing that they went fast so they didn't have to suffer," or "You'll see them again." I tried to believe I would see them again, but I knew it would not be in *my* lifetime—and their passing didn't feel like a blessing to me! What I had appreciated most was the silent squeeze of an empathetic hand, an arm around my shoulder, or just a big hug.

Downstairs was where Mom stored her treasures. Pop hoped she might have stored the life insurance there. Mom had organized everything in a neat system— everything had its box, and each box had a label. We started digging. Soon, I found myself uncovering some wonderful stuff that I had nearly forgotten.

At the bottom of the ART box I happened on a folder filled with some of my earliest renderings. It was simply labeled HANNIBAL'S KINDERGARTEN PICTURES.

The art was standard kindergarten—nothing special. Nevertheless, Mom had cached them all in a neat little folder. At nine, I was a little embarrassed at the quality. I could do much better now, I thought. Still, each creation included a lovingly placed silver star in the upper right-hand corner with the words "good job" written underneath. Mom had pasted the stars and penned the words. It hadn't mattered to me much how my teacher graded my efforts because Mom thought I was the most talented artist ever born. I wasn't, of course, but she sincerely thought so, and I was rewarded every time.

In my later years, now being very wise, I realized that Mom was visionary. She didn't see the pictures, she saw a picture of my life—my possibilities. She envisioned who I was and who I could become. Somehow she could project past the poor drawings to the potential that hibernated within me. I could never see it. So she imaged that vision to me, giving me enough light to see where I should go, and ultimately enough light to see where I had been.

I dug a little deeper into the folder. I remembered this artwork. I had painted a picture of our house—my first watercolor, now stiff and wrinkled from the dried wash. I had been so thrilled with it. When I first brought it home and presented it to Mom, she was speechless. She hugged and praised me for what seemed an hour, telling me over and over how proud she was. Then came the ceremonious placing of the star and the words "*very good job.*" But that wasn't all. This time Mom made some of her famous chocolate chip cookies for dessert—

the pancake-sized ones—and Dad taped the picture to a prominent display area on our refrigerator door, where it hung for a month. After that, the refrigerator door became my own personal art gallery.

Now, all that remained of the reward was *"very* good job." The star was gone, but I could see the outline where it had once been stuck. Still, clutching that simple, poor picture flooded me with memories of how Mom always regarded my smallest accomplishments as superior. And she really believed them so. I could never fail completely because Mom's faith in me was too strong. Oh, I stumbled, sure, and I made some of the dumbest mistakes a person ever could. Mom thought I was great, though, and that was enough to set me upright, dust me off, bind my wounds, and start me over again.

It's a wonderful thing to be okay. Once in a while an uninspired character would tell me I wasn't. But, when I felt the worst, Mom would hold me and listen, and, in the end, I had my *star* and enough determination to go on.

I replaced the contents, secured the lid, and slid the box back to its place. An adjacent one was labeled CLOTHES. At this point I was finding more interest in the memories than the elusive policy. I pulled out the box and removed the lid.

The thing that makes clothes smell old is mothballs. Mom believed in them, and they seemed to have worked. As far as I could determine there was not one moth in the entire box of clothing. Why in the world had she stored all these things, I wondered. Furthermore, if these clothes *could* be worn again, how would you ever get the smell out? As I surveyed the contents of the box and then reviewed the number left to search, I quickly became convinced that Mom had never thrown away anything in her life! And everything had been boxed, labeled, and pickled in mothballs.

On top lay a little, light blue, short-sleeved shirt, and fastened to it, a black snap-on bow tie. When we moved to our home in Nampa, an aunt had given me this outfit to wear for the first day I attended our new church—and Mom had saved it. As I lifted it from the box, I noticed a button missing and a large rip where the button should have been. I remembered.

"Hey, Todd. There's that new kid." A ruffian named Roy crowed as if he were talking to his accomplice, but he was obviously directing his taunt to me. He pointed a mocking finger at me. "Hey, kid! Is that the only shirt you got? Look, Todd. He's wearing that sissy shirt his *mommy* dressed him in."

It had never occurred to me that the shirt was sissyish. Actually, I was proud of it. Suddenly, though, I was sandwiched in by the two older boys—one in front of me and one in back. I couldn't move. The one in the front appeared pretty tough. He was. When I stammered for an adequate comeback to his query about the number of shirts I owned, he took it as a stall and lifted me by my shirt to meet him face-on. I was never a large boy, but I weighed enough to cause what happened next—an immediate terrible ripping sound. I promptly fell from Roy's grasp. The shirt was ruined. Given the choice between revenge or life, I chose life. But still, I had a difficult situation to defuse. Dad had earlier given me a wonderful gift that I could draw upon for this very type of predicament.

My father once asked me, after a similar scrimmage, if I knew what a *peacemaker* was. I didn't.

"That's someone who loves to make peace more than to fight," he coached.

"How do you 'make peace,' Dad?" I asked.

He answered with a question. "If someone does something really bad to you, do you know how to walk away without fighting?"

"They'd call me a sissy."

"That's just a word. Because they call you a sissy, does that make you one?" Dad pressed.

"Well, no. But what can I do?"

"Son, you *always* have a choice. No one can *make* you do anything." He followed with a question that was difficult for a little boy to understand. "Who has the most courage: the one who fights and calls names, or the one who is silent and walks away?"

"I know what you're going to say," I said, "but it sounds hard."

"It sometimes *is* hard, but would you rather go through life fighting? Here's the hardest part. A peacemaker learns to *love* his enemy."

"What if someone is going to hurt me?" I asked.

"You must defend yourself, of course, but in almost every situation you have a choice. If you can, try to be a peacemaker first. Remember, son, it takes two to fight."

It takes two to fight. As I stared up at Roy and Todd from the ground, Dad's words from a calmer moment echoed through my mind. Well, then, I wouldn't—fight.

I stood. I looked those bullies straight in the navels and said, "Hey, guys, wanna play football?"

They studied me, totally taken aback, shrugged their shoulders, and said, "Sure." So we played football for an hour and had the time of our lives, with Dad and Mom keeping a distant surveillance the whole time. I suppose Dad could have stopped the bullying at the first confrontation, but he was wiser—and for the price of a shirt and button I had learned one of the most valuable lessons of my life.

At 2:00 P.M. we were hungry. Pop and I made our

way back upstairs to the kitchen. Mom still had valuable pieces of art displayed on the refrigerator door. My last picture was a drawing of our family—all stick people of various sizes, with the caption, "Dad, Mom, Hannibal." I guessed Mom had liked it, because there it hung on the refrigerator door with a star in the upper right-hand corner.

Pop had brought some sandwiches, and we found some canned fruit in the cupboard. Then we retired to the living room for lunch.

Mom always kept a variety of magazines by her easy chair. Dad and Mom kept the family Bible on the coffee table. They never used a bookmark to remember where they had been reading, or a pen to mark special passages—they just tore off backs of envelopes and jotted down special references and thoughts and stuck them in the Bible at the appropriate pages. Intrigued, I picked up the Bible in one hand and my sandwich in the other. I scanned the onionskin pages, stopping occasionally, trying to understand some of the big words and uncommon phrases. As I thumbed through, the torn flap of an envelope fell onto the floor with the reference Isaiah 49:15,16.

"What's this, Pop?" I asked, retrieving the scrap and handing it to my grandfather.

He squinted at the scrawling. "Well," he said, "let's

look it up."

Pop turned the pages until he found the right spot. "Here it is," he said. He read aloud the words, "'I will not forget thee. Behold, I have graven thee upon the palms of my hands.'"

"What does that mean?" I said, leaning over to look at the passage.

Pop pondered a moment and said, "I guess it means that when you feel all alone and everything seems hopeless, there's always someone who loves you completely—someone who will never leave you no matter what you have done."

"Like you, Pop?" I asked.

"You know I will always love you, Hannibal," he responded, "but I've come to believe that a greater love exists than we humans often feel—a perfect love that means you would give everything, even your life, for someone else. That's the kind of love you can't repay."

I think Pop soon decided that my mind was too small for such big thoughts. So he told me a story instead.

⬝⬝⬝

"Once there was a father who had two sons— one good and one bad—whom he loved dearly. Although he was very poor, the father crafted a beautiful golden pendant with a sculpted soaring dove on its face. He made it round like a sand dollar, and he cut it into two pieces, exactly down the middle, so that it split the image of the bird. Bound together, it became whole and the dove was complete and seemed to hang there like a cloud—its delicate wings catching beams of light and reflecting golden rays in every direction. It was beautiful. When the pendant was finished, the father set the pieces on golden chains and hung them around his sons' necks.

" 'Your strength is that you are bound together like this pendant,' he said.

"The younger brother—the bad one—thought it all so much foolishness and hated working on his father's farm. Times were tough. The little family needed help from each member. Early one morning, just like other mornings, the father woke his younger son with the familiar words, 'Time to water.'

" 'But it's still dark!' the boy complained.

" 'Plants don't care. Let's go.'

"An hour later, the younger brother reluctantly arrived in the field. He worked until the hot sun rose, and kept at it all day, working and cursing, clearing the ditches ahead of the water. It ran quickly. Sweat poured off his head and into his eyes. He swung his shovel and watched the water racing by and thought he felt his life was racing by. Water swelled in the blisters on his hands. Anger swelled up inside his heart. He looked up the field toward the setting sun and saw his father and brother toiling side by side, laughing together and loving their work.

"That was it. He threw his shovel down and sprinted from the field to the house, where he emptied into his pocket the savings for next year's seed, threw some clothes into a pillowcase, and stomped to the door. Slamming the door behind him, he cleared the porch steps with a stride and hit the ground running. There was no looking back, and it was much too soon for regrets. He raced down the road into the twilight. He thought he was finally happy.

"Over time, he found his way into a big city, where he felt a little awkward at first, but his money bought him a lot of fake respect. There he lived a wild life, spending the money freely on bad friends and worse pleasures. It wasn't long before he woke up one morning broke. That was the biggest surprise of his life.

"The second biggest surprise came when he realized he was in jail. He couldn't remember getting there. These were times when you could get sent to prison just for owing people money, and this boy owed a lot. The prison officers told him that if he would pay his debts and pay for the damage he'd caused the night before—he couldn't even remember where he'd been the night before—the charges would be dropped. But if every cent wasn't paid, he'd be in prison for a long, long time.

"For many days the prisoner sat in the filth of the prison and longed to hope again. He was struck with as great a fear as he had ever known—the fear that he had passed the point of help. He sat in the bitter darkness racked with inexpressible torment for what had brought him to this. Nothing was hidden. He remembered it all— every gross deed, every foul moment of his debased, immoral past. There were no more excuses, no more justifying wrongful acts, no more shifting blame. He felt like the sod on his father's farm when it was being harrowed and broken, exposing all that was hidden underneath to the terrible open gaze of every onlooker. If there is a hell, he thought, this was surely it, and he was a child of it. He longed for the relief of death, but even that was not enough. Oh, he thought, that I could just cease to exist. Thus, for many days he sat in the prison and suffered the exquisite pains of a damned soul. Then, when he felt he could endure no more, he remembered his father and brother, and the tiniest glimmer of hope sprouted within him. Would they take him back? Could they help him?

"When his father received the news of his son's

troubles, he grieved. He loved the boy, although some might have said he had little reason to. But he also was glad, because his son wanted to come home, even if it was for the wrong reasons. He called his older son to him, and together they tried to work out a plan to pay the enormous sum that was needed.

"The older son finally said, 'I can sell my twenty acres and the dairy cows I own. If I put those funds with the money I've saved, it should be enough to free him from prison—and, if I must, I will sell my pendant.' The father burst into tears at his son's willingness to sacrifice so much. The older brother was offering to give everything to save his brother. Both the father and his oldest son were weeping when the firstborn left to rescue his brother.

"The faithful son trudged the long distance alone. He didn't know how his younger brother would react to his coming. When he came to the prison he negotiated a price with the warden, and the older brother was given the key to his brother's cell. Alone, he descended into the deep parts of the prison, past the filth, the liars, cheaters, and murderers, down to the deepest corner, where he found his brother. He turned the key and swung open the prison door.

" 'You're free, brother,' he said, and stretched out his hand. 'Come follow me home.'

"Can you imagine the younger brother's joy when

he first stepped back into the light of day? Only those who have been bound in the shackles of their own making can appreciate the sudden relief of liberty. The older brother proved his love by giving his all. Try as you might, Hannibal, you can never repay that kind of debt. All you can do is remember and do better."

———

Pop finished by saying that my mom and dad had always trusted in God and loved me with that same kind of unselfish love.

We stood to leave. We hadn't found the insurance policy. Pop said he expected we wouldn't. As I surveyed the old house once more, familiar emotions stabbed my consciousness and haunting questions remained unanswered: Where do I go from here? How do I fill this huge hole in my life? In a real way, a big part of me died when my parents did. I looked around one last time trying to find something substantial I could take with me to fill the hollowness. Pop fastened the padlock to the front door and walked me to the pickup.

"It's too late to sell brooms today," he remarked. "Don't feel much like it anyway."

As we drove off I turned back to take one last look at the only home my parents had owned. It seemed to weep in loneliness for the ones it had sheltered so long and so well. When I sat back in the seat, Pop put out his big hand and patted me on my knee. Then, without saying a word, he stuffed an envelope into my palm. "Hannibal" was written on the front side. I looked at him questioningly, but he just stared straight ahead as he drove down the road. I carefully lifted the envelope, tore it open at the top, and spilled the contents into my cupped hand. There lay a tarnished silver star, a button with some blue thread hanging from it, and a torn piece of paper with the handwritten reference Isaiah 49:15,16.

It was nearly dark when we drove away. I looked out in the distance to see the evening star climb the horizon. I sat for a moment in silent contemplation, then dropped my treasure back into the envelope and put it in my pocket. I was leaving with an answer. I had some pieces of my mom and dad woven together, as it were, with a silken thread. And somehow those seemed like enough.

◆ ◆ ◆

OSCAR,
I LOVE YOU

THE OAK BOX STILL lay on Pop's fireplace mantel untouched. I shouldn't have told Charlie about the treasure inside. He wanted to open it. So did I. But I forbade him and I resisted. The furnace didn't heave and groan in the summertime, but its home was still as frightening. Charlie's father had lately settled into a particularly bad mood, so Charlie and I spent a lot of time together—especially sleeping outdoors.

In Boise, when air-conditioning was just a notion for the rich, boys slept out more than in. To say that we *slept* is more than a little inaccurate. Mostly we roamed the neighborhood searching for some mischief. Charlie taught me the fine art of garden raiding. I hadn't sampled too many raw vegetables before, and they tasted particularly sweet when mixed with a little larceny. Charlie knew how to play poker, too—strip poker. Once we concocted a rule that the defeated had to jump out of his sleeping bag and, at the whim of the winner, do a jig, hang by his heels from a tree limb, or perform some other proof of losership. But we never enforced it. We hid in our sleeping bags when we lost. We weren't bold enough for more daring exhibitions.

I thought of these activities as innocent enough until one day Charlie joked, "What if your grandpa were here watching us?" We laughed, but later I thought that maybe I shouldn't do things that I wouldn't want Pop to see. Still, Charlie was older and I often found myself following him into new and uncertain territory.

One sleepout morning Charlie and I woke to the shrieks of Charlie's cat, Samantha. Mr. Bennett had risen early and was stuffing each of her newborn kittens into a gunnysack with the purpose of tossing the sack into the Ridenbaugh Canal. Charlie had seen this before.

"Dad, stop!" Charlie yelled as he bolted from his sleeping bag and ran to rescue the babies.

Just as quickly I heard the slamming of our screen door and Pop yelling for Mr. Bennett to wait. I watched the goings-on safely from my sleeping bag. After an exchange of words and money, Mr. Bennett relented and handed the sack of kittens to Pop. Then Charlie, Samantha, and I followed Pop into our house, where he set the kittens in a warm, safe spot and placed Samantha with them in great contentment.

Later, when Pop, Charlie, and I were discussing the incident over breakfast, Samantha entered the kitchen with a large, fat dead mouse in her mouth. I jumped back and Charlie started for his cat, apologizing to Pop. But Pop stopped him with a gesture. Samantha surveyed the room with a singleness of purpose until she located the man who had saved her children. She then walked to him and laid the mouse at his feet.

"That's disgusting!" I said. But Pop stared with reverent awe at the cat, and then reached out to lift her to his lap, stroked her back, and scratched her behind the ears. After a moment, he set her down and she slipped away to tend her kittens.

Pop then picked up the mouse with a napkin, procured a spade outside the back screen door, and buried the mouse in his garden. When he returned to finish his breakfast, he asked us boys, "What did you think of Samantha's gift?"

"What gift?" Charlie hooted. "It was just a mouse, for goodness' sake!"

"Yes," Pop responded, "but it wasn't just any mouse; it was a fat, magnificent mouse—one of the best specimens I've seen. How do you think Samantha feels about it?"

I spoke up. "She thinks it's wonderful."

"Exactly so," said Pop. "Try as you might, some

debts can never be repaid. But this cat was grateful and gave the best she could. Always remembering is payment enough."

෴

One day in mid-July, Mr. and Mrs. Davies asked Charlie and me to tend their farm while they left on a weekend trip to Nyssa, Oregon. We knew we were big then. We were to shoulder the responsibility of the whole farm—a singular charge for young boys.

On the second day, after feeding the chickens and being bested by Gertrude, we decided we had earned a break. Charlie and I bounded to the haystack, where he managed to stay throned on Bunker's Hill for a full half hour—a self-proclaimed new record, he calculated. I conceded. Then we climbed up through the hay-walled tunnels until we stood side by side on the brim of our fort. Nothing could have prepared us for what we saw.

Mr. Davies's constant warning had been to watch the calves so that they didn't escape their pen and get to the alfalfa field. To our dismay, one had—my Oscar. We didn't know how long Oscar had been eating the tender green alfalfa leaves. But, from the bloating, he had been there a long while.

"Get Pop!" I cried to Charlie. Charlie took off and I

tried to hold on to Oscar so that he couldn't move. Mr. Davies had explained to us boys that cattle can't belch. So, when they eat green alfalfa, their stomachs rapidly fill with trapped gas, and without relief, the animal can die.

Oscar soon began to panic because of his terrible pain. He bawled and bolted from side to side. Tears streaked my face as I begged God to save my pet. Somehow I clung to him long enough for Pop and Charlie to come running.

"He's dying, Pop!" I screamed. "Help him!"

"Get in front of him and hold his head, Hannibal," Pop directed. "Charlie, you help!" I grabbed Oscar's head and held him as tightly as I could. Charlie held Oscar around his neck. "No matter what happens, don't let go!" Pop ordered. Then he pulled his pocketknife from his pocket and thrust the blade between the calf's ribs into its stomach. Gas and blood gushed from the wound like a burst balloon. Oscar bellowed and tried to escape, but we held on. I had never smelled such a foul odor. Then, just when I thought I would faint from the stench, Oscar's legs gave way and he collapsed to the ground, panting and bellowing.

With Pop's help, we managed to lift Oscar into Pop's pickup and carry the crying calf to a holding pen in Mr. Davies's barn.

"Now we wait," Pop said.

That night Pop offered to camp with me in the barn. I accepted. My soul hurt. I knew Oscar was suffering because I had not watched.

Through my tears I blurted, "I prayed for God to save Oscar. If he dies I'll never believe in him again!"

Pop sat quietly a moment, then asked, "So God exists only when things go your way? You can't imagine him away. Do you think that punishing God will make you feel better?"

He was right, of course, but my little boy's heart couldn't push past the pain. "I prayed for Mom and Dad to live and they didn't."

"I know, Hannibal," Pop said. "I did, too. But just because God doesn't answer your prayers the way you want doesn't mean he's not there. If every prayer were answered our way, there would be little purpose to life. What good would there be if we could just pray and all our trials and mistakes would magically vanish? Doesn't sound like much of a life to me. And I doubt that most of us really know what's best for us, anyway. Pain and consequences are part of life; that's part of being here. Without pain, life would be pointless. We should pray for God to help us understand our pain, not for him to take it away.

"I once knew a man from New Meadows who told

me that he hadn't believed in God since he was a boy. He told me that when he was a little boy his father had given him the job to herd horses from a high mountain pasture to a lower corral. As he was moving the horses, they became spooked and started running out of control. He said that he ran as far and as fast as he could, but it was useless. So, he said, he fell on his knees and prayed for God to stop the horses. When I asked him what happened next, he said that two men appeared from the woods, caught the horses, and brought them to the corral. Then he said—and this is the clincher—'I haven't believed in God since.' I couldn't believe my ears! I told him that I had seldom heard a more miraculous demonstration of God's existence. But he said, 'Well, it wasn't God who stopped those horses. Thank goodness those two men were there to help.' Now, I suppose we can all go through life trying to outguess God, or telling him how we think things should be or how he ought to be running things, but when everything is said and done, God doesn't have anything to prove. He's not the one on trial."

Neither Pop nor I slept. We nursed the weak, sick calf late into the night. Mr. and Mrs. Davies returned home about five o'clock, just when the first hint of morning burst on the broad Idaho sky. Pop asked me to stay with Oscar while he went to talk to his neighbors. Mrs. Davies stepped into the house with her suitcase, and the two old gentlemen came over to inspect the calf.

Mr. Davies was kind. He wasn't angry as I had expected. He could see I was hurting. He bent down and tenderly examined Oscar, then at length he arose and turned to Pop, directing his conclusion. "I've had some experience with this," he started. "This calf is in misery. There's nothing we can do to save it. We'd best end it quickly and keep it from suffering more. I'll do it. You'd best take the boy home."

Pop nodded. He put both hands on my two shoulders and said, "There's a hard job that's got to be done here, Hannibal. Mr. Davies thinks it would be best if we leave him to take care of things."

I knew they were right. I buried my head in the neck of my Oscar and wept. Finally, I stood on my nine-year-old feet and, with as much courage as I could muster, said, "Mr. Davies, you gave Oscar to me. He's my calf. I made the mistake. I'll take care of it."

Both men looked at each other for a sign. Then Pop said, "It's okay, Henry."

Mr. Davies returned from his house with a rifle and a box of shells. "Do you know how to use this, son?" he asked.

"Yes, sir," I replied. But I wished my answer could

have been different.

Mr. Davies loaded one cartridge and handed the rifle to me. "Between the eyes," he softly instructed as he stepped back. I took the rifle and aimed it at my friend. Then, lowering the barrel a moment, I whispered, "I love you, Oscar." One shot later and Oscar's misery ended.

It was to be five months and two weeks before I held a gun again.

◆ ◆ ◆

A LIE

SCHOOL DOORS OPENED IN September. An early burst of cold had turned the leaves brilliant hues of red and yellow, uncommon for Idaho's late summer. I had entered the fourth grade. Charlie should have been in the fifth, but his father wouldn't allow him to attend. Charlie brushed it off as if he didn't care. I knew better. He spent lonesome days waiting for school to end so we could play.

Once, when we were fishing, I asked Pop if fish felt pain when they were caught. He understood my question because he had watched me observe the sudden spasm and shuddering of a just-hooked worm, and the flopping and wrenching of a trout on my line. He told me that we tend to measure pain by the amount of noise coming from the suffering. He said he supposed if fish could scream there would be fewer fishermen.

Charlie was like a hooked trout. No one heard his hushed hurting.

Late in October Charlie showed me a way to jimmy a window in the school gymnasium. This was not the first time Charlie had introduced me to fringe activities. My following him into more and more questionable adventures was fast becoming a tightening, strangling noose around my conscience. On the one hand, I was his only friend and he mine. On the other hand, I knew what we were doing was wrong. Pop used to say that he had no use for anyone who did wrong knowingly. What Charlie and I did was wrong, and I knew it.

That day Charlie and I snuck into the empty school building and shot baskets for an hour or two before we heard the distant echoed footsteps of someone coming. "Quick. Upstairs!" Charlie whispered. We doused the lights, dashed to the upstairs lavatory, and closed the door.

"Be quiet!" Charlie said, poking me. I tried to swallow my pantings and gaspings. We crouched in deep silence for what seemed forever, until Charlie calculated that the coast was clear. Slowly, I rose, cracked the door, and peered out into the hall. Nothing.

"Look out the window," I whispered, motioning. Charlie tiptoed over to the lavatory window and surveyed the grounds below.

"Hannibal, come see this," he said, bidding me to

join him. Two stories below, Mr. Jackson, our school's custodian, stood examining the very window we had earlier negotiated.

"We're dead!" I cried. "There's no way out!"

We slumped to the floor. Neither of us could think of a door or window that wasn't bolted or secured. We were trapped. Suddenly, Charlie popped up. "I've got it!" he blurted as he pulled a balloon from his trouser pocket. "Get ready to run!"

I divined his objective when I saw him fill the balloon with water from the sink. "We'll never make it!" I said, shaking my head in desperation.

"Sure we will!"

"No, we won't." But it was too late. Charlie had taken aim, and the sloshing orb was launched and falling toward its target.

Mr. Jackson would have been better served if he hadn't heard the shuffling noise above, and looked up just as the globe struck him dead center on the bridge of his nose.

"Communists!" he shrieked, and before we could make our escape we heard the advancing footsteps of a soaked custodian. We hadn't counted on Mr. Jackson's speed.

"Block the door!" Charlie cried. "Put your back against the door and brace your feet on the wall."

Imminent death is a motivator. I was small, but somehow I managed to wedge myself between the door and the wall while Mr. Jackson pounded and bellowed from the other side. When that failed, we heard him back up a few paces, then run full speed and throw himself at the door like a human battering ram.

"Charlie!" I screamed.

"I'm thinking! I'm thinking!" Charlie said as he paced.

"Well, think faster. He's going to kill us!"

All at once Charlie said, "The next time he hits the door move out of the way . . . and be ready to run!"

I didn't have time to protest. While Mr. Jackson backed up to charge the door again, Charlie lifted me off the floor. "Get ready!" he said. We heard the heavy thuds of Mr. Jackson's feet as he rushed the door. Then, at the precise moment, Charlie reached out and opened the door. The fuming custodian crashed into the room, bounced off the wall, and fell backward, sprawling on the floor.

We didn't look back except once as Mr. Jackson chased us down the stairs, swinging his broom like a sword-carrying gladiator. I ran fastest that day, and Charlie received a sound swatting to the back of his head. Luckily for us, in his rage Mr. Jackson had left the gymnasium door wide open for our getaway. He pursued us a bit, but soon gave up to boys who were in much better condition and had more at stake. As we rounded the schoolhouse I checked behind me to see a red-faced, dripping figure hunched over with hands on his knees, trying to catch his breath. He raised himself with what strength he had left to shake a clinched fist in our direction as we raced into a nearby field and lost ourselves in the high yellow cornstalks.

When I arrived home late for supper, Pop asked where I had been. "Playing on the street with Charlie," I told him. Pop said he had called for me, but I hadn't answered. "Sorry," I said. "Guess I didn't hear you." Pop eyed me a little but didn't press. This was my first intentional lie. It fell from my mouth awkwardly but fully alive, and it stuck to me like a leech.

At dinner, I pushed around some brussels sprouts, trying to feel better. I soon discovered that I felt worse about the lie than the breaking in. Pop could see that I was willing to starve before I ate the repulsive vegetables, so he made me an Arkansas favorite—cornbread and milk. That night I worked on times tables by the warmth of the fireplace, and Pop read Mark Twain. Our evening turned to night without a word passing between us.

When I rose for breakfast the next morning, Pop had been awake for several hours and had prepared eggs and bacon. He hustled around the kitchen whistling "Ol' Dan Tucker" as though nothing had happened the night before. "You going to play with Charlie again today?" he asked.

"I expect so," I replied.

"What adventure you got planned today?"

"Oh, I guess we'll go over to the Davieses' like we did yesterday," I said without thinking. For one horrifying moment I realized that I couldn't remember where I had told Pop I had been yesterday and why I had come home late.

Pop stood still and thought a moment. "I thought you said you spent yesterday playing on the street."

I was caught, so I said the first thing that came to my mind. "Oh, did I say yesterday? Must've been the day before."

"You mean yesterday you were at the Davieses' and the day before you were playing on the street?" he asked, sitting down next to me.

"Yeah . . . uh, I mean, no. Yesterday . . ." But I couldn't remember what I had said before. So finally I blurted, "Why does it matter anyway?"

"It doesn't if you're telling the truth," he replied.

"What makes you think I'm not?" I asked defensively.

"Because you're no good at it."

"No good at what?" I challenged.

"Telling a lie," Pop stated.

I knew I was caught.

Then Pop gave me a quick course in lie telling. "If you're going to tell a lie, you'd better have a good memory. A lie is an interesting thing. It doesn't have a life of its own. It takes its life from you. You bring it to life by telling it in the first place. And the only way you can keep your lie alive is by telling another. Problem is, you have to remember them all. You brought the lie to life, you see, and you're the only one who can keep it going. The truth, on the other hand, has its own life. It exists forever and never changes. You don't have to remember anything. So, Hannibal, have you told the truth?"

I hadn't and I was ashamed. I broke down and told him everything, and to my surprise he lifted me onto his lap and told me he was proud of me for coming clean. He was serious long enough to ask if I had learned a lesson and to tell me that I should apologize to Mr. Jackson. Then, when he was convinced that I was sufficiently repentant, we had a big laugh. "I've done worse," he chuckled. But I didn't believe it. He patted me on the head and told me to go play and have fun.

As I started for the door, he sobered just once more with the urging that I should never lie again—that lying to the liar is like alcohol to the alcoholic. "Remember, Hannibal," he said, "the test of integrity is whether it's for sale. Don't sell yours, son, not even for a tiny lie."

◆ ◆ ◆

Things Forbidden

HALLOWEEN BROODED OVER BOISE with eerie expectation. I decided to trick-or-treat as a hillbilly. Pop was amused. He gave me one of his old felt hats and showed me how to fashion it like a true Razorback. First, we tore off the band and soaked the hat in water until it was thoroughly saturated. Then we draped it over the end of a broom handle and stretched it on all sides until it was long and pointed. It was a moonshiner's hat for sure. I placed it on my head, pulled it down to eye level, and suddenly I stood a full twelve inches taller. The rest of my backwoodsman's garb was comprised of torn Levis, a red-checkered shirt, and a bandanna. I wanted to go barefoot, but Pop thought better of it.

Charlie showed up at 6:00 P.M. as a bleeding monster with a bolt through his head. After Pop photographed us, we bounded out the door at 6:05 P.M.

to fill our pillowcases with wonderful treats. What I didn't know was that Charlie had planned a trick. We canvassed two streets before I found out.

"Wait for me here," Charlie said. "I'll be right back." He ducked under a barbed wire fence and disappeared into the Davieses' barnyard. Before long, he returned with a full paper sack and a jar of something liquid. He motioned me into an empty irrigation ditch, and when he was sure we were alone, he popped open the bag.

"That's disgusting!" I yelled, as I peered down at a fresh cow pie. "What's that for?"

"Shhh! You'll see" was all he would say.

Charlie slipped behind trees and bushes as he crept to a strategic location. I followed behind, irritated but intrigued. Soon Charlie dropped to his knees behind a picket fence and signaled me to do the same. "That's ol' man Jackson's house," he whispered.

"Hey," I rebutted, "we're already in enough trouble. Let's get out of here."

"Not until I get him back for hitting me with his broom," Charlie said defiantly. "You going to help?"

"What do you mean?"

"Look," Charlie explained. "We'll hurry up to his house like we're trick-or-treating. Then I'll take the sack and drop it on the step. You pour this jar of gas on it and I'll light it."

"Wait a minute!" I interrupted. "Where'd you get the gasoline?"

"Stole it," he bragged.

"Who from?" I challenged.

"What does it matter? I've stolen lots of things."

I couldn't believe my ears. "You're lying! I've never seen you steal anything."

"Well, I have," Charlie countered. "What do you think I do when you guys are in your fancy school? Me and Dad do it. He checks out places, I sneak in and get the stuff he tells me, and Dad pays me money to do it. I tell you, there's no feeling like it. Now are you going to help or not?"

I shook my head. Charlie called me a wimp, but I knew I wasn't. Then he dashed away to Mr. Jackson's porch.

He was all alone when he dropped the sack, doused it with fuel, lit it with a match, rang the doorbell, and ran for cover. In an instant, Mr. Jackson sprang to the porch, stamping out the flames, flinging manure all over himself, his house, and everything in range.

Charlie laughed until he was sick, but I was scared. "Come on!" I insisted, pulling Charlie away from the scene as quickly as I could.

We left trick-or-treating and we sprinted to my house. "I'm going inside to warm up," I said.

Charlie followed me, still laughing. "Be quiet," I

shushed him. "Pop will hear you." But Pop had left a note that he had gone and would be back soon. Charlie decided to count his candy and warm up by the fire before going out again. I closed the front-room blinds and turned off the lights on the porch and those inside the house. I was certain Mr. Jackson had followed us. Charlie said there was no way Mr. Jackson could have known who did it or where we had gone. But I was not so easily convinced.

At that moment the furnace moaned, and both Charlie and I straightened in fright. Distant sounds of trick-or-treaters echoed down the street, and our fire sent strange forbidding shadows bouncing off the walls. We dared not move. A small gust of wind blew open the back screen door, and it slammed against the side of the house. Tree limbs scratched anxious, bony fingers on the front-room window like fingernails dragged across a chalkboard.

Suddenly, we heard the sound of a breaking branch. We crouched in hushed apprehension. "He's out there!" I whispered.

"He couldn't be," Charlie objected. "I was gone before he came to the door. He couldn't have seen me."

"Maybe he followed us," I argued. There was only one way to find out. "You stay here and listen," I ordered. "I'll go out the back door, sneak around the side of the house, and see if anyone is there."

The once-brave Charlie didn't object to my plan. I saw him shrink into a corner while I crawled through the house to the back entrance. The screen door was old and rusted and held in place with a spring stretched from the door frame to a hook in its middle. There was nothing quiet about it, but, aside from the front door, it was the only way out.

The ancient hinges groaned with every movement. And as I pushed the door open, the spring made a terrible grinding noise. After what seemed like hours, I stepped past the door and inched my way around the side of the house to the front. When I was close, I fell to my stomach and quietly drew myself forward until I could see the yard. I scanned the property for signs of any concealed intruder. My view was partially blocked by some foliage at the base of the front-room window, but, after waiting and carefully listening for any sinister movement, I felt sure that, except for me, the yard was vacant. That determination, though, didn't alter my returning as cautiously as I had come.

I knew Charlie would be relieved to hear my report, but what I saw when I entered the front room made me weak in the knees. Charlie had taken down the old oak box from atop the fireplace mantel.

"Put that back!" I screamed, rushing to grab it from him.

"Take it easy," Charlie countered, placing himself between me and the box. "Come on, let's take a look," he urged. "When will we ever get another chance?"

My mistake was considering his proposition. Charlie was right, I reckoned. I never would get another opportunity like this, and I had wanted to see the treasure for so long. I decided I could look, put it back, and no one would be the wiser. These were the thoughts that prepared me to tell my second lie. Pop was right: lying is an addiction—once begun, it is hard to stop.

I knew I would feel better if I made conditions, so I bravely gave a command. "Okay, but I'll hold it. You just stay back." Charlie consented and handed me the box.

The fleeting thought that what we were about to do was wrong flickered in my mind, but it was soon extinguished by my consuming desire to at last discover the treasure in the box. I lifted the golden hasp and gently raised the lid. There on the smoothed oak surface lay an old photograph of a young man in bib overalls, posing with a shovel and irrigation boots, standing in front of a big barn.

"The treasure must be underneath," Charlie determined. I agreed and set the photo aside. Just as we had suspected, the picture covered a keyhole that housed a compartment in the bottom of the box.

"Open it," Charlie said excitedly.

"There's no key," I responded, checking the sides, the bottom, and the underside of the lid.

"The treasure has got to be in there!" Charlie said in a loud voice. "Where would your grandfather keep the key?"

Before I could think, we heard a sudden scratching at the window. I motioned for Charlie to lie low. We took turns gesturing at each other to creep to the window and look outside. Charlie lay frozen when the sound returned, so I knew that by default I had been elected. I inched toward the window and warily parted the blinds. What I saw caused me to collapse in a paralyzed heap. There, in the window, I saw Mr. Bennett, Charlie's father, staring at me . . . and the box. Almost immediately the headlights of Pop's pickup signaled his return, and Mr. Bennett vanished into the night.

Charlie escaped from the house through the back. I managed to replace the photograph, fasten the hasp, and heft the box to its former position. When Pop entered the house, I wanted to confess and tell him about Mr. Bennett. But, when I tried, the words caught in my throat. I knew this time I had done something terribly wrong. All I could think to do was live silently with my deed, which is the worst lie of all.

◆ ◆ ◆

Our Last Adventure

WHAT WE DO FOR love is the subject of many a tragic tale. The Charlie I had known in recent days was not the fun-loving boy who shared my summer. Pop said if love is food for the soul, we will fiercely fight for its nourishing embrace. Charlie was no different. In his lonely hours he allowed himself to play a dangerous game, one he could never win—to gain his father's love and approval. Charlie had learned to rob, lie, and cheat for him, hoping that one fraction of affection might be measured in return. But all he accomplished was to feed his father's habits and enable his gross addictions. Like the abandoned chick I left in June, Charlie hungered for meat but fared on crumbs. He was slowly dying.

Charlie's visits became less frequent by my resolve. I loved him as much, but couldn't abide his lifestyle. That we had split on a forked road was becoming

painfully apparent. Something else kept me from him—
the pang of fear I felt knowing that Charlie and his
father had seen the box and had admired it. Charlie
knew stealing now and bragged that he was good at it. I
wrestled with the uncertainty of wondering if I, his
truest friend, might be his next victim. Within the
month my fears would be realized, and thus began our
most harrowing adventure together.

December brought a crisp chill to Boise's atmosphere,
and a thin blanket of snow. The promise of Christmas
with its bright colors and cheery music dogged my
senses and heightened my anticipation. Broom business
was brisk. Some saw in them gifts, but most needed to
replenish their summer-worn bristles with newer and
stronger ones for the harsh winter coming. If he could
wait for school to end for the day, Pop would take me
selling; if he could not, I tarried at home alone until he
returned in the evening. On those cold, lonesome nights
I amused myself at the fireplace hearth, warming my
body with a woolen blanket and rehearsing Pop's stories
to the dancing flames. I didn't touch the box that sat
above me on the mantel. I knew where the furnace was,
and I remained far from its mournful lamentations.

Christmas Eve 1960 was such a night. Pop had left
early that morning to deliver brooms in Emmett, then he
was to bring home a tree that we would trim together. I

had cleaned the house, as he had asked, and wrapped some presents for tomorrow. I expected that Pop would love the dinner I had waiting for him—cornbread and milk, Arkansas style. According to the weatherman the sun had set later that night than the night before— we had passed the winter equinox—but I thought everything looked just about the same. Pop and I had strung some popcorn and draped a paper chain through the house, adding to the festive spirit. Pop had made my first Christmas in his house special and fun. He knew I still hurt from recent memories, and his intent was to have as nice a Christmas as we could. He would be home soon. A fire would be cozy, I thought, as I reached for the kindling.

But abruptly, as I huddled in my blanket, a terrible unfamiliar noise echoed from the furnace room. I frightened to my feet and stood silently listening for the sound's return. What I had long supposed about the basement was most certainly true, I feared, for a moment later the chilling sound recurred with greater intensity. I crouched on my knees and crawled to the entrance of the staircase, straining at every awful sound. The basement door was open. I slipped behind it so that I could peer below through the crack where the door hinges to the frame. In the far corner I could see the beam of a flashlight pierce the stale darkness.

Suddenly, a jarring, screeching sound straightened me upright against the wall. Someone was forcing open the basement window!

If I concentrated, I could just make out whispered words.

"Push it open!"

"I can't. It's stuck!"

"Give me the crowbar, then!" A fearsome creaking followed. "A little wider and you can crawl through. There. Now, feet first and drop to the floor."

"Don't make me do it. It's too far. I'll break my leg!"

"I'll break your neck if you don't! Get in there, Charlie!"

Charlie! I couldn't believe what I was hearing. My best friend was breaking into my house! And I knew why. "Where is Pop?" I screamed inside.

Then I heard Charlie say, "What if somebody sees us? Or what if someone is home?"

"Quit stalling," Mr. Bennett threatened. "The car has been gone all day." Then came a dreadful crashing sound. "Charlie, what was that?!"

"I fell and knocked over some paint cans. It's too dark to see. I'm okay, though, and I'm in!"

"Good! Open the cellar door."

Charlie did just as his father asked. He fumbled until he found the lock, released the bolt, and pushed open the door.

"Now, hide outdoors and watch to see if anyone's coming," Charlie's father ordered. Charlie obeyed and slipped into the winter night to wait and watch.

When Mr. Bennett appeared in the doorway, he was carrying the crowbar he had used to jimmy the basement window. He waved it to his right and then to his left like a weapon. I knew then that his purpose was unswerving—he intended to have the box and its treasure without thought of consequence or cost.

I had little time to think. My heart pounded wildly. I knew if Pop were to return and surprise or challenge the thief that he might certainly lose his life. Mr. Bennett skulked to the stairway and began his deliberate, silent ascent. All I could think to do was press my body against the wall behind the door and stay as still as possible.

When Mr. Bennett mounted the top stair, he lurked a moment as he surveyed our front room, searching for the oak box. If he had looked left he would have spotted my frightened eyes not one foot away. As it was, he stood close enough for me to smell his foul odor and the stink of liquor on his breath. I held mine, aware that even the opening and closing of my eyelids might give me away and bring a swift end to my life.

Mr. Bennett soon located the fireplace mantel and

moved toward it. I knew my only chance was to escape below to the dark shadows of the ghastly furnace room—and my only chance for protection was to get Pop's gun! I slipped from my hiding place as Mr. Bennett removed the box from the mantel. I quietly descended the stairs when he stopped to inspect his prize. Of this much I was certain: I had never before known as fearful a place as the one I was in; I had never before known the terrifying possibility of death.

Suddenly, I recognized a sound outside. Pop had returned. My terror increased. Mr. Bennett stalled in the living room to take account of his circumstance. I heard him make for the stairs. How I managed what came next I don't know. In my fright I had the presence of mind to find Pop's twelve-gauge shotgun and point it up the stairway—without a shell in the chamber.

When Mr. Bennett stood two steps from the basement floor, I summoned what courage I could and shouted loudly, "Halt where you are. I have a gun!"

He stopped short. "Who's there?" he snarled, peering into the darkness.

"Never mind," I answered in a quivering voice. "You just put that box down or . . . or, I'll shoot."

Mr. Bennett was slick. "That's you, isn't it, Hannibal?" he said sweetly.

"Yes," I stammered. "I won't let you take Pop's box.

Put it down."

"Now, son, I wasn't going to take it. I just wanted to look at it." His oily lie leaked from his mouth. "What did you say about a gun?"

"I've got one and I know how to use it!"

"Let's see it." Mr. Bennett was shrewd. His attempt to gain my trust was transparent, though, and I didn't move from the shadowy hole where I was hidden.

He shifted a little to his right. "Oh, there you are." I shrank into the corner, doing my best to heft the heavy gun and hold it steady on its target. "Say, that is a beauty," he said flatteringly, as he inched toward me.

"Stand back!" I shouted. "Just put the box down now!"

Mr. Bennett bristled at my command. "I thought we were friends. You come to my house. You play with my boy. I treat you like kin. And now you stand there with your silly gun pointed at me and accuse me of stealing this worthless old box. You've got some nerve!" He cursed something I had never before heard.

I marshaled all the courage I could and demanded once more, "Put down the box and get out of here!" Just then, Pop hollered from outside for me to open the front door so he could bring in the tree.

"You drop that gun, boy," hissed Mr. Bennett, "or I'll kill that old man right now and then I'll get you." I held firm, shaking, trying to steady the shotgun. Mr. Bennett looked anxiously back toward Pop's voice, then at my shotgun. "You ain't got the guts, boy," he taunted. "Now you give that to me."

Pop yelled again. "Hannibal! Come help me!"

"Well," Mr. Bennett resolved, "let's see what you've got." Then he raised the crowbar and lunged at me like a crazy man.

All I could think to do was throw the gun at him. He didn't see it coming. The barrel caught him in the throat and his feet tripped over the stock, sending him sprawling on the basement floor. I grabbed the box he had dropped in his fall, and cowered back into the shadows. Then I heard Pop shouting from outside and pounding on the locked front door. Mr. Bennett lay reeling on the floor, coughing and gasping for air. I felt tears gush from my eyes as I tried to muster the courage to leap over the stunned thief and run upstairs.

Finally, I made myself do it—I bolted for the stairway. I hadn't taken the second step before a rush of pain shot through my leg and I fell forward. I looked behind me and saw Mr. Bennett's gloved hand wrapped around my ankle. "I'll get you now," he swore as he damned me with an oath. I screamed in fright and pain, wrenching and twisting with all my strength to tear myself loose from the madman. Suddenly, I heard a loud thud and I was loosed from his grasp. I didn't turn back until I had bounded up the stairs and heard a pitiful groan.

"Run, Hannibal," I heard from the dark. Then I turned to see Charlie standing with a piece of lumber in his hand. "Run." And he was gone.

◆ ◆ ◆

THE
MOURNING DOVE

LIFE HAS A WAY OF smoothing and shaping our rough edges, like a stone thrown into the current of a raging river. At first we tumble and roll with every crashing wave until we are polished and rounded. Then we settle where we are not moved as the torrent roars and the waters wash over us.

For the next two hours our house was filled with confusion. Pop held my poor shaking body as I sobbed each detail to the constable. I watched them bring the shackled and bandaged Mr. Bennett from the basement, then hustle him away. Charlie was taken in a separate car.

When all had left I whispered to Pop, "Aren't they taking me to jail?"

"No. Of course not," he replied, surprised. "What in the world are you talking about?"

"Well," I started, "it's all my fault. Don't you see? I

was the one who let Charlie look at the box. If I hadn't, this all might not have happened. I'm just as guilty. Don't you go to jail for that?"

Pop could see I was hurting and confused. "No one's to blame but Mr. Bennett for his greed."

"But I've done so many things that are wrong. I don't want to live this way anymore. I'm bad and I don't know if I can ever be good." I wasn't trying to be dramatic—I really believed what I was saying. Try as I might, I could not recall anything good about myself. I felt a sense of hopelessness settle over me like a fog. My conscience hurt more with every remembered detail of my past weeks' mistakes. Pop tried to bring everything into perspective, but my judgment had become skewed beyond repair.

"You remember the story you told me about the boy whose brother rescued him from jail?" I asked to make my point. "Well, if that were me, he should have left me in there to die!"

Pop sat me on the floor in front of him, wrapped me in a blanket, and said, "I know you feel bad right now. I can see why. But you've got to know how much you are loved and how good you really are." I began to protest, but he continued. "If you'll let me, I'll tell you some more of that story." I was too upset to argue. Pop began.

II The prisoner was grateful, but also embarrassed and ashamed of what he had done, and how he must look to his brother who had freed him. He didn't offer any resistance, but lowered his head and never spoke a word all the way home. The evening sun was setting on the dusty road as the two brothers came in sight of the old farmhouse. In a far-off field, they saw their father working, but he didn't see them.

" 'Come and eat,' offered the older brother. 'Father will be in soon.'

" 'I don't think I can just yet. How can I face him?' And the younger brother turned into the barn to avoid his father's notice. His brother followed him. 'Come in. Please. You have to know that Father loves you. We both love you! We want you home. That's all that needs to be said. That's all that will be said.'

"The old barn was dark and cool inside. The younger boy fell into the freshly thrown straw and wept in pain. His older brother lit a lantern and knelt beside him. After a while, the younger lifted his face to his brother's and said, 'I'm so ashamed. How can I ever repay you for what you've done for me?'

" 'Remembering's enough' was all the older answered.

" 'Remember?' The younger felt the waves of guilt flow through his body. 'All I remember is the damage I've done and the hurt I've caused. I can't get it out of my mind.' He thought about how stupid, how selfish he'd been. His whole life lay exposed like an open wound. He was feeling just about crazy when he grabbed the lantern. He screamed, 'How can you even stand to look at me?' and threw it against the wall.

"An explosion of flame burst on the dry old boards, and raced along the dripping kerosene through the straw to the mangers, running with impossible speed. The two brothers whipped off their jackets and beat at the fire, but the flames rose higher, hotter, and the barn filled with thick, choking smoke.

"From the field their father saw the black clouds belching from the windows and door of the barn. He immediately left his work and raced toward the blaze. His two sons inside fought the flames like wild men. Then the younger brother's lungs filled with smoke and he fell unconscious. The older brother, seeing that the barn was lost, dropped to his brother's side, grabbed his arms, and tried to drag him to safety. When the father got to the barn door, he could barely see his sons through the swirling flames and he shouted encouragement. But his oldest son also collapsed, overcome by exhaustion and lack of air.

"The father tried again and again to run into the barn, but the searing heat drove him back. He called to his sons frantically, but received no answer. Then he heard a terrible rending groan. He looked up and the barn roof staggered crazily, leaning in on twisting, burning joists and collapsing walls. He grabbed a horse blanket off the fence, plunged it elbow-deep into the water trough, and stumbled into the barn with the wet blanket around him. The heat knocked him to his knees, but he crawled toward his sons, groping his way through the blinding smoke. Finally he found one, then the other.

"He wiped aside his tears and squinted into the faces of his boys. Suddenly, the roof exploded in a shower of embers and began to crumble and slide toward them. He had only one awful moment—time to pull one boy out. But which one? Which to live? Which to die? It was a choice no mortal ought to have to face. 'O Heavenly Father,' he cried. 'Help me!' And he clutched one of his limp sons and dragged him into the cool night air as the barn collapsed in a terrible ruin of flame and death behind him."

❧

Pop went quiet. I hardly noticed. The fire hissed and popped, and Pop's rocking chair creaked softly. But I was still hearing the rush of flames in the barn, the roar of the collapse. Then I realized how dark it was. But neither of us got up to turn on a light or lay a log on the fire. I just sat, waiting. The story had filled me up, held me, hurt me.

The old wooden floor groaned under Pop's rocker. My leg had gone to sleep, and I straightened it. I knew the story couldn't be over yet, and I looked up into Pop's face, looking for an ending. But he just rocked and rocked, staring into the tiny flames.

"Pop?" Still the old man rocked in silence. "Pop, go on with the story. Who did the father save?" I touched my grandfather's knee. He started. I looked up at him again, still waiting. He raised his eyebrows. "What?"

"Who did the father save?" I asked a little louder.

Pop stared off at the ceiling and started rocking again. "Does it matter? Either way he saved a life, and that life was his son."

"Of course it matters! What's the use of telling the story anyway if you don't tell how it ends? Come on! Don't do this to me!"

"Why don't you finish this one, Hannibal?"

"Pop, don't tease me! I've been through enough today."

Pop stopped rocking and leaned toward me. "I'm not teasing. How would you end the story? How would you like to make a decision like that? Someday you'll have kids of your own. Let me tell you, no matter what they do, you'll love each one fiercely."

Pop let this work on me a little, then he said, "I recall once last summer you had to make a choice a little like that."

I winced a little. I closed my eyes and saw feathers and smelled gunpowder.

"What did you think about then? Can you tell me?"

I didn't want to remember. But he was asking me to remember more—more than I had already. I guess the dark of the room helped me feel a little more safe, kind of hidden from the truth, a little less ashamed. "You mean the doves, don't you." It wasn't a question. I knew he meant the doves.

"Well, it was a little different, y'know. The two chicks, well . . . they were both good . . . not like in the story." I was choking back some feelings, getting a little embarrassed. "They both had pinfeathers." Now tears were rising. But Pop was listening. I knew I had to go on.

"I didn't want to just do it like they were nothing. I mean, I wanted them to know how I felt!"

"How did you feel, Hannibal?" Pop asked.

I was going to cry pretty soon. It was harder to talk. "I spoke to them," I said softly. "I spoke to each one. The one I was going to kill I held in my hand . . . .Oh, Pop! It stretched up and opened its mouth like I had some food or something! It didn't know what was going to happen."

"What did you say to it, Hannibal?"

"I told it I was sorry. I was really sorry. But I don't think it understood. How could it have known that I had picked it to die? The other one I left in the nest. I didn't want it to smell like my hands. Maybe its father would be afraid of it."

"That was wise, Hannibal."

"I talked to the little chick in the nest. I said, 'Little bird, you gotta promise to live. You gotta promise to grow up strong and sing and fly.' "

I was crying hard. I didn't wonder if Pop thought I was strange to talk that way to a little bird. He just listened thoughtfully.

After a few moments, I composed myself enough to choke out one more thought. "I want to go back to the field next spring and see if he's there. I want to see if he has grown big and beautiful, if he has a mate and a family."

Pop didn't often cry during storytelling. I guess that's another reason why I suddenly felt uncomfortable being the storyteller instead of him. I wanted his voice back again. "Pop, now you finish your story. Which of the two boys did the father save?"

Pop studied my face. "Hannibal," he said quietly, "the father saved the younger son. He left the older one in the barn."

"Why?" I couldn't believe it. "Why would he do that? It's not fair! The older boy was so good and did everything his father wanted. How could the father leave him in the barn to die?"

"The father lived for one purpose, Hannibal—to give life to his sons. He couldn't make a decision like that based on love alone—he loved both his sons equally. He had to make his decision based on something greater than love. Don't you see? The younger son was the one who needed to learn the sacred lessons of life. He needed time and a chance to change."

The moonlight spilled through the window onto Pop's silver hair. He looked older then than I had ever remembered. It hit me that he wouldn't be around forever. I felt genuinely sad, looking up at him, watching him rock quietly as he stared into the fire. How many more of these evenings would we share together? What a gift this man was to me. I couldn't imagine a world without his love. In a real way he had saved me.

"Pop?" His eyes shifted to mine. "Pop, tell me about the younger son. What became of him? Did the father make the right choice? Did the boy change?"

"He was given the chance, son. That's the thing."

I knew I couldn't ask again. The story was over, but I felt unsettled. I stretched out my leg—it was asleep again. My tears had about dried. I wasn't afraid or hurting anymore.

Pop had stood to put a new log on the dying fire. I watched him lean over the rising glow. He fumbled about the fireplace a little, then he said, "You still don't understand, do you?" I shook my head, but he didn't turn to see me. I heard the distant chimes of a church bell. I looked at the clock. It was Christmas day, and all was calm and bright. Like the soft music breaking through the still air, I could imagine such a night long ago when the only sound echoing on Judea's plains was a mother's lullaby hushing her baby's cries. I remembered that Pop had said when men try to change the world they send an army, but when God changes the world he sends a babe. The distant Christmas bells chimed the promise of life that such a babe brought— the promise of love, the promise of hope and joy.

Pop poked at the fire, then turned until his glistening eyes met mine.

The firelight glinted off the pendant around his neck, two golden halves bound together, embracing the full image of a dove in flight. At once I felt the purest love I'd ever known. I understood his story.

◆ ◆ ◆

About the Author

LARRY BARKDULL has been a publisher of books, magazines, music, and art prints for twenty years. *The Mourning Dove* is his first book. His second book, *The Touch of the Master's Hand*, will be published by Golden Books. He lives in Orem, Utah, with his wife, Elizabeth, and their ten children.